S0-DYD-552

New Firsts

by DIANA GALLAGHER

STONE ARCH BOOKS
a capstone imprint

CLAUDIA AND MONICA: FRESHMAN GIRLS
ARE PUBLISHED BY STONE ARCH BOOKS
A CAPSTONE IMPRINT
1710 ROE CREST DRIVE
NORTH MANKATO, MN 56003

LIBRARY OF CONGRESS CATALOGING-IN-PUBLICATION DATA

GALLAGHER, DIANA G.
  NEW FIRSTS / BY DIANA G. GALLAGHER.
     P. CM. -- (CLAUDIA AND MONICA, FRESHMAN GIRLS)
  SUMMARY: CLAUDIA AND MONICA ARE BRAND NEW FRESHMEN
AT PINE CREEK HIGH, AND THEY ARE FINDING THAT RELATIONSHIPS
SOMETIMES CHANGE AS YOU GROW UP--WILL HIGH SCHOOL PULL
THEM APART OR WILL THEY REMAIN BEST FRIENDS?
  ISBN 978-1-4342-3275-5 (LIBRARY BINDING)
  1. HIGH SCHOOLS--JUVENILE FICTION. 2. DATING (SOCIAL
CUSTOMS)--JUVENILE FICTION. 3. BEST FRIENDS--JUVENILE FICTION.
4. FRIENDSHIP--JUVENILE FICTION. [1. HIGH SCHOOLS--FICTION. 2.
DATING (SOCIAL CUSTOMS)--FICTION. 3. SCHOOLS--FICTION. 4. BEST
FRIENDS--FICTION. 5. FRIENDSHIP--FICTION.] I. TITLE.
  PZ7.G13543NE 2012
  813.6--DC23

                              2011032816

GRAPHIC DESIGNER: KAY FRASER
PRODUCTION SPECIALIST: MICHELLE BIEDSCHEID
ART CREDITS FOR COVER AND INTERIORS: SHUTTERSTOCK

PRINTED IN THE UNITED STATES OF AMERICA IN
NORTH MANKATO, MINNESOTA.
062012   6798R

CLAUDIA & *Monica:* FRESHMAN GIRLS

We've been friends forever.
And now we're in high school.
Two best friends,
getting ready to face
the world of boys,
homework, tests, romance,
and growing up.

Thank goodness we have each other.

CHAPTER 1

CLAUDIA

Finally. I'm in high school. Or I will be next week, anyway. And on the Thursday before school starts when I walk into Pine Creek High for Orientation, I feel like jumping for joy. But I don't.

I can't wait to look around the new school and check out my class schedule, and I want to see my friends. It's a fresh start for all of us, and I'm going to make the most of it—starting with a makeover.

This is the perfect chance to start over, to be the person I want to be.

I'm not getting plastic surgery or going on

What Not to Wear or anything. I'm just paying more attention and being more careful than I was before. I bought a bunch of new makeup, and Mom gave me money for new clothes. I'll be at the mall all day Saturday.

I even trimmed a few inches off my long, curly hair. Ugh, that was so hard to do! I kept my eyes closed the whole time, but the split ends had to go. They were starting to frizz. My hair still falls halfway down my back, but the new style makes me look older and shows off my eyes.

But looking more grown-up is only part of the new me. I don't want to seem like a baby. Especially to all the older kids. Word about the kids in the new freshman class will spread fast after Orientation. The lobby is full of older student volunteers.

A cute boy with sandy blond hair and a sticker name tag that reads ANDREW is standing just inside the front doors. He smiles. "Welcome to Pine Creek High," he says.

"Thanks." I smile back, and feel my face warm up.

I hope he can't tell that I'm blushing.

"The volunteers over there have the class lists," Andrew says, pointing toward the tables against the back wall. "Orientation is held in your homeroom. They'll tell you where to go."

I don't see anyone I know, but the line moves quickly. In less than five minutes, I'm standing in front of a girl named Coral.

"I'm Claudia Cortez," I tell her.

Coral runs her finger down an alphabetical list. "Here you are. Your first period class is your homeroom, too. You have American History with Mr. Harris in room 248."

"Where is that?" I ask.

"Nobody knows!" the boy sitting beside Coral says.

Coral laughs. "That's why they gave us a map," she says.

The school campus is brand new for everyone— not just the freshmen. The school boards in the towns of Pine Tree and Rock Creek decided to replace Pine Tree High, which was too small, and Rock Creek High, which was too old, with one big facility. It cost less and has everything high school students could want—except maybe peace and harmony in the halls.

Pine Tree and Rock Creek have been arch rivals forever—about everything. Building one school was money smart, but throwing hundreds of hostile teenagers together? Not so much.

Thanks to Monica Murray, my best friend since third grade, I know a few kids from Rock Creek. Monica, Chloe Granger, and Rory Weber all ride at the same stable. Still, I have never cheered for Rock Creek to win a football game, and I don't have any friends from there. It's still too weird to imagine us all getting along.

Coral points to a printed floor plan that's taped to the table. "Straight down the front hall, take the first right and go up the stairs to the second floor. Then just follow the signs," she tells me.

I want to find out if Monica is in my homeroom. But before I can, Coral shouts, "Next!" The boy behind me moves up, and I leave to find room 248.

The building smells like fresh paint, and everything looks new. The floors aren't scuffed, and the metal lockers are shiny, not scratched with graffiti. The small windows in the classroom doors are clean, and the black lettering on the hall signs is easy to read.

I pause outside the classroom door to take a deep breath. I want everyone to notice how much more mature I seem, but I don't want to be too obvious or fake.

I take another deep breath and walk through the door. But my grand entrance comes to an abrupt halt. Before I have a chance to scan the room for friends, I hear a dreaded laugh.

Anna Dunlap, the bossy supreme ruler of Pine Tree Middle who made life miserable for everyone who wasn't in her circle of friends, is sitting right in the front row.

Anna has never liked me. She's always wanted
Brad Turino to be her boyfriend, and she hates the
fact that he and I are on the verge of being a couple.
Apparently, that breaks the rule that football players
are only supposed to hang out with cheerleaders
and other football players.

Gina Tanner walks right in front of me. She's a
sophomore, and two years ago, when she still went
to Pine Tree Middle, she was the head cheerleader.
She's handing out class schedules.

"Hi, Gina," Anna says. She's all lit up, expecting
Gina to be thrilled to see her. They used to cheer
together, but Gina is a year older than we are. I'm
not sure her middle-school cheer camaraderie will
translate to high school. Is it horrible that I hope it
won't, as a matter of fact?

"Where did you get that awful bag?" Gina asks
Anna.

"It's a Ginger Snap," Anna shoots back. "They're
very expensive."

"And the envy of all the little girls in middle

school, I'm sure," Gina says. She hands Anna her papers. "Here you go."

I don't like Gina's snotty attitude, but I can't help laughing. Anna says and does things that are just as mean and cruel all the time. She treats everyone like dirt, even her best friends.

I expect her to say something snotty. Instead, she just snatches the papers out of Gina's hand and gets up to find a different seat.

That's when I see Brad. When Anna dashes for the empty desk beside him.

Typical Anna Dunlap. But the twinge of jealousy I feel goes away when Brad catches my eye. His face lights up with a smile and he points to the empty seat behind him.

"Save it for me," I say, but there's no way he can hear me. Anna starts talking—the only way she knows how, too loud—and he's too polite to ignore her.

I don't want Anna to think I'm worried she's stealing Brad—I'm not, really—so I glance around the room. Monica isn't there, but I wave to my friends Adam Locke and Tommy Patterson.

"What's up, Claud?" Adam says.

"You got taller," I say, smiling at him. It's true. Adam's looking a lot more man-like all of a sudden, instead of the scrawny middle-school kid I knew.

As soon as I have my schedule, I bolt for the desk behind Brad. "Hi," I say, sliding into the seat. I hang my bag on the corner of the chair. I want to compare my schedule with Brad's, to see how many classes we have together.

Brad looks back and smiles. "How's it going, Claudia?" he asks.

"Great!" I exclaim. "I can't believe we're in the same home—"

"None of my friends are!" Anna interrupts me. She places her hand on Brad's arm and winks. "Except you."

"Maybe you'll have other classes with Carly," Brad says.

Anna sighs. "I really hope so. But I was counting on homeroom," she says.

"I know how you feel," I say. "I don't know if Monica's in this homeroom or not."

Brad says, "I don't know half the kids in here."

"They're from Rock Creek," Anna says, rolling her eyes. "Not worth knowing."

"Some of the Rock Creek guys I met at football practice were pretty cool," Brad says quietly.

"How did practice go?" I ask.

Anna interrupts again, like I'm not there. "Some might have been cool, but not most, I bet."

Brad frowns. "The Rock Creek kids probably feel the same way about going to school with us."

"You're right," Anna says.

"I know," Brad says, smiling at her.

I frown. Normally, I wouldn't care that Anna was flirting with Brad. Anna flirts with everyone. But he's acting like I don't exist, and he's flirting back.

All right. I know that Brad and I aren't an official couple, but it still hurts to see him flirting with another girl. It feels like he's cheating on me. Which I know is dumb, but I can't help it.

Our teacher walks in.

"Wow. I hope Mr. Harris is as nice as he looks," Anna says, raising an eyebrow.

With a slim build and a bit of gray in his dark hair, Mr. Harris is kind of good-looking. Okay, he's more than kind of good-looking. But I couldn't care less about that. I want an A in American History.

"I just hope he's a good teacher," I say. Anna doesn't respond.

Brad waves at a tall, muscular guy walking into the room. "Hey, Tyler!"

The guy gives Brad a quick nod, but he doesn't sit near us. Anna asks, "Who's that?"

"Tyler Brooks," Brad explains. "He plays football. He used to be on the Rock Creek team."

Tyler sits down on the other side of the room. That's when I notice that the classroom is equally split: Pine Tree on one side and Rock Creek on the other.

The desks on either side of me are both empty. I put my bag on one of them to save it. But as the minutes pass, I lose hope that Monica will walk through the door. I can handle high school. But can I handle it without my best friend?

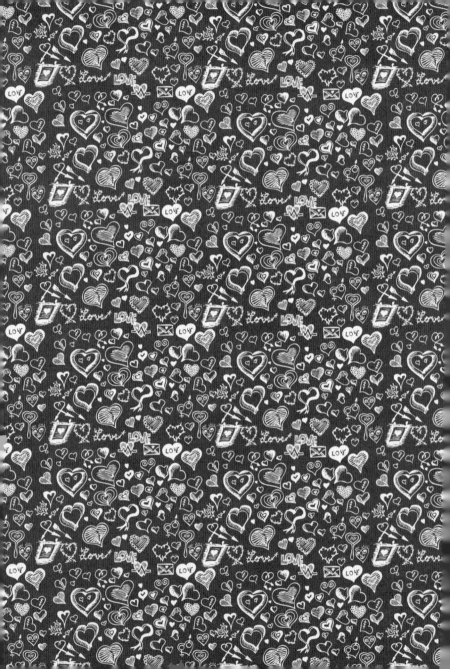

CHAPTER 2

Monica

I don't want to start high school making excuses. I doubt Mr. Harris really cares why Chloe and I were late tonight. He doesn't want to hear the whole stupid saga about how my mom and stepdad were busy, my grandpa got stuck in traffic, and Chloe's mom was late to pick me up, and then we had no clue where anything was in the new building. Mr. Harris just wants us to show up. So we're running through the halls of Pine Creek High, trying to find our classroom.

When we finally find the room, we slow down. I walk through the door just as Mr. Harris stands up.

"Yes!" Claudia shouts from the back of the room. I smile and wave.

"You're just in time," Mr. Harris tells us. "Pick up your schedules and find a seat."

Gina hands us our schedules and checks our names off on an attendance sheet. She gives the paper to the teacher. Chloe and I sit on either side of Claudia.

"You're here!" Claudia whispers.

"So are you!" I whisper back.

Brad gives Claudia and me a thumbs-up. The mythical Brad Turino, suddenly just a regular guy. Claudia has been in love with him for as long as I can remember. They started hanging out last year, so we're all friends now. And they're totally in love, even if they don't quite know it yet.

"Looks like everyone is here," Mr. Harris says.

"Everyone but Carly and Karen," Anna Dunlap mutters. She's sitting in front of me.

Carly Madison and Karen Chen are Anna's best

friends. Claudia and I aren't part of her popular crowd. She's awful, but I still feel sorry for her.

"Raise your hands if you went to Rock Creek Middle," Mr. Harris says.

All the hands on one side of the room go up. Chloe is the only Rock Creek kid sitting on the Pine Tree side. Her face turns red right away.

"I know Pine Tree and Rock Creek have been rivals for a long time," the teacher says. "But you're all Pine Creek Panthers now. Mingle or I'll assign seats!"

A wave of grumbling ripples through the room. But everyone gets up and shifts around a little bit. Brad squeezes Claudia's hand before going over to sit with some Rock Creek football-player types.

I have Rock Creek friends, so mingling doesn't bother me. But it might be a problem for the athletes and cheerleaders. They totally despise each other.

Mr. Harris doesn't waste time telling us the

school rules. We can read the handbook online. He says, "My big rule is that I don't mind if you guys take notes on your phones. It seems inefficient and slow to me, but whatever works for you."

Everyone smiles. But Mr. Harris's face gets stern. "However, if a phone rings in class, or if there's obvious game-playing or texting, it's mine till the end of the day. No exceptions. Two times and you're out. Any questions?"

Anna raises her hand. "When do we sign up for extracurriculars?" she asks. "Like cheerleading."

"Great question. Check the list of clubs on the school website and sign up on your school account," Mr. Harris says. "You have until Tuesday afternoon to decide. You can sign up for three, but you must sign up for at least one."

"Is band a club?" a boy from Rock Creek asks.

"Both," Mr. Harris says. "Band, chorus, and drama club are classes and clubs. If you get into them, your schedule might change. The rest of the clubs meet after school. I don't know the rules about trying out for cheerleading, but I imagine all of that information is online."

Gina clears her throat. "It's not like the other clubs," she says. "You actually have to try out. But no freshmen are allowed. There's a special freshman tryout at the end of the year. We do a lot of work over the summer."

"And there you have it," Mr. Harris says, smiling at Gina. "Cheerleading. Not like other clubs, apparently." Anna slumps in her chair.

"Do we have to audition for band and chorus?" Tommy asks. He's usually the class clown, so I'm surprised that he's acting quiet and calm for once.

"Yes, for both," Mr. Harris says. He glances up at the clock. "All right. You have an hour to look around before you leave. I'll see you all next week. Be on time!"

"What clubs are you going to sign up for, Brad?" Anna asks as we all walk toward the door.

Claudia and I look at each other and roll our eyes. Anna doesn't care about clubs. She just wants Brad's attention. Even though it's clearly on Claudia. I guess she forgot that Claudia won the battle for Brad two years ago.

"I haven't really thought about it," Brad says. "I want to make Varsity on the football team, but freshmen almost never do."

"You will," Claudia says. "You're the best quarterback ever." We head out and stand in a group just outside the door.

"I can't believe freshmen aren't allowed to try out to be cheerleaders," Anna says. "I'm sure I'd make the squad."

"No, you wouldn't," Gina says, walking up.

"What?" Anna looks shocked.

I bite my lip so I don't grin. I've never seen Anna being insulted to her face. There is always a price to pay, and it's always horrible. The rumors she starts are the worst. She can be really nasty.

"I'm the only sophomore on the squad. And that almost never happens, either," Gina says.

Anna looks crushed when Gina walks away. I try to take the sting out. "You'll make the squad next year, Anna. Seriously, don't worry about it. Gina's just being . . . Gina."

Anna looks back with a scowl. "I don't need your pity, Monica."

Chloe starts to laugh and covers her mouth. She's never had to deal with Anna before, so she's probably shocked. Anna just storms away.

We all watch her leave. "That was intense," Chloe says.

I shake my head. "That was typical Anna Dunlap," I say. "You haven't seen the worst of it by any means."

"Well, I hope I don't have to," Chloe says. "Now, come on. Let's check this place out."

"Do you want to walk around with us, Brad?" Claudia asks.

"I wish I could," Brad says. "The team is meeting at the gym. But if I don't catch up before you leave, I'll call you later."

"Oh, okay," Claudia says. "See you later." She watches sadly as Brad walks away. Weird.

Standing close to her, I suddenly realize that she's wearing more makeup than normal. She's got perfect skin and thick, dark eyelashes—no reason to coat her face with makeup. Also weird. Maybe she's been breaking out a lot, or something.

She notices me staring at her. "What?" she asks.

"Oh, nothing," I say, smiling. "Where should we go first?"

"Let's go find our lockers," Chloe says. "The numbers are on our schedules."

The hall is full of kids checking room numbers and schedules. As we walk, we compare our schedules. Claudia, Chloe, and I don't have all the same classes together, but we have a few.

"When do you have lunch?" Chloe asks.

"Fifth period," Claudia and I say together.

"Me too!" Chloe grins. "Thank goodness. I thought I'd be stuck eating all by myself in a corner, or something. I'd have to join the gamer club just to have someone to sit with."

"What clubs do you want to join?" I ask.

"I don't know. There isn't a horse club," Chloe says. "I checked."

"I don't mind that," I say. "I'm still going to ride, but
I don't think I'll spend as much time on it as I used to."

"Really? Are you still going to take lessons?" Chloe asks, looking worried.

"Of course," I say. "But I'm not going to have time to get out there every single day."

"Yeah, I guess there's going to be a lot of stuff to do besides ride," Chloe says. "I'm thinking about trying to join chorus, maybe."

"Dad wants me to pick clubs that will help me get into college," Claudia says.

I laugh. "Of course he does," I say. Claudia's dad is so big on getting into college, even though we're only freshmen. I copy his deep voice and add, "Claudia! Your television programs will be available forever on the internet, but your homework is due tomorrow! Television won't get you into Harvard, you know!"

Chloe and Claudia laugh.

"Anyway, clubs," I say. "I really don't know. I didn't know you HAD to pick one. And what was that business about if you get in?"

"Juniors and seniors get first choice," a familiar voice says from behind us.

When I spin around, I see my best guy friend in the world, Rory.

Side note. Rory's more than my best guy friend. He's also the guy I have a huge crush on. We've known each other for a few years.

I give him a big hug. Then I step back and notice that he's wearing my favorite T-shirt, a worn Bad Dog concert shirt. He looks as happy to see me as I am to see him.

"Hi, Rory," Chloe says. Then she frowns. "Wait a second. So we join any club we want? Or what?"

"Not if it's full," Rory says. "Just hope you don't get stuck in something awful if your top choice is taken."

"What are you doing here, anyway? Sophomores don't have to be here, and I thought you weren't helping with Orientation. Were you looking for us?" I ask.

"Absolutely," Rory says, winking at me. "Friends have to look out for each other, right?"

"Right," I agree, smiling back at him. "That's exactly what all good friends do."

I can feel Chloe giving me a look, but I won't look back. She thinks Rory and I are meant to be. Like, in a romantic sense.

Okay. If I'm being perfectly honest, so do I.

But this is real life, and I don't think I have a chance. Rory's so cute and sweet and he's a great guy, but he's also a sophomore, a football star, and the lead singer in one of Pine Creek's coolest bands. Basically, he's a catch. And I'm a nobody.

And we're friends. Like he said.

Still, it can't hurt to have an adorable, popular football player as a best friend!

"We're trying to find our lockers," Claudia says.

"What are your numbers?" Rory asks. We show him our schedules, and he leads us down the brightly colored hall to the huge bank of freshman lockers.

I can't believe it. More good luck! Only one locker separates me from Chloe. Claudia's locker is right across the hall—two down from Brad and right next to Anna.

So while Orientation started off bad, things are looking up.

And when I look up, all I see is Rory.

CHAPTER 3

CLAUDIA

It's Monday morning. Specifically, twenty minutes past the time I planned to be completely ready for school. And I can't decide what to wear!

I never had this problem in middle school. I always looked okay, obviously, but not like I should be a model or anything. Not like Anna. For the first time ever, I realize that I could use her advice now.

As I'm staring at my closet, a horrible thought hits me, and I freeze.

What if Brad meets someone he likes better? Someone who knows how to dress and wear makeup perfectly and do all the right high school stuff?

He's never actually asked me to be his girlfriend, and there's more competition this year. All the Rock Creek girls are new. Not to mention all the older girls.

I'm almost totally, absolutely positive that I don't have anything to worry about.

But just to be sure, I have to look fantastic.

I bought a few new outfits at the mall on Saturday. It took hours, but the clothes are perfect. Or at least I think they are. Before I start second-guessing my shopping, I decide to just close my eyes and pick a hanger.

By the time I'm finally ready, I don't have a single minute to spare.

"Let's go, Claud," my brother Jimmy says. "I'm not waiting. Come right now or you can take the bus."

"Okay!" I say.

As I rush toward the door, Mom yells, "Claudia! You have to eat!"

"I will!" I shout. But I'm too excited-slash-nervous-slash-terrified to eat. I just shove a banana in my bag and run.

Monica and Chloe are already there when I make it to homeroom. They saved me a seat, and put Chloe in the middle so Mr. Harris won't make us move. Chloe's from Rock Creek, so technically, we're mingling!

"I love your top, Claudia!" Chloe exclaims. "Where did you get it?"

I can barely remember what clothes I put on. I look down. I'm wearing a light blue tank decorated with simple embroidery, and my favorite jeans. "The Grab Bag, at the mall," I say.

"I love their stuff," Monica says.

"I was there all afternoon on Saturday, and—" The words catch in my throat when Brad walks in.

Should I wave Brad over to the empty seat beside me or let him pick? My mind zooms.

I don't want to act like I own him. Like I said,

I'm not even really his girlfriend. But if I play it cool, he might think I'm mad or not interested or something.

I decide to wave, but it's too late. Anna Dunlap beats me to it!

"Brad!" Anna calls from the back of the room. She's sitting by herself. "Can I talk to you a minute?"

Brad glances at me and shrugs, like he doesn't have a choice. Then he goes to see Anna.

I hate her perfect hair.

I wish Anna would find a guy that's not already taken, but that's not her style. Stealing boyfriends is more fun.

Then Jenny Pinski takes the empty desk I was saving for Brad. "I'm so mad I could spit," she says. "This stupid school doesn't have a girls' wrestling team. Should I talk to the coach?"

"Absolutely," I say. "It can't hurt."

I look back, and Brad is sitting next to Anna.

I can't concentrate on American History because I'm thinking about Brad. Monica thinks that boys don't make a move unless they know—for sure without a doubt know—that a girl wants to be with them. Being friends isn't enough. Somehow, I have to let Brad know I want to be his girlfriend without actually telling him I want to be his girlfriend. Telling him would feel too pathetic, like I was begging him. That's the last thing I want.

But the thing I want the most is to be Brad Turino's girlfriend.

Before the bell rings, I copy down the homework assignment and hope I didn't miss too much.

"I wish you had second period English with Chloe and me," Monica says.

"Yeah, me too," I say. I start picking up my books, but I'm watching Brad so I can time my exit just right. When he starts walking toward the door behind Anna, I cut across two rows of desks.

I have it all worked out in my head. I'll ease into line behind Brad and stay with him until we have to split off for second period. That way Anna won't have won. Not entirely, anyway.

Second period I have General Science with Mrs. Marino. Brad is in Monica's English class, but I don't remember the room number.

I'll ask. That can be part of the plan. That's how I'll steal his attention away from Anna.

You know what's not part of the plan? Tripping over a chair leg and crashing right into Brad's back.

Brad stumbles and pushes Anna, who yelps and moves out of the way. When she looks back at me, she rolls her eyes. "You're such a klutz, Claudia," she says.

"No way," Brad tells me. "You're adorable."

I smile. Anna looks disgusted and keeps walking. Brad puts his hand on my waist to let me go ahead of him.

"Where's your next class?" I ask.

"English," Brad says. "I'm not sure where it is, though."

"I think it's at the other end of the school," I say. "You better hurry."

Brad winks at me and rushes toward the stairs.

Anna stands in the middle of the hall. She spots me and waves a map of the school. "Where's Room 127?" she asks.

I happen to know, because my next class is in Room 127 too.

"I have General Science next too," I say. "I know how to get there."

"Great," Anna says. "Let's go."

Anna doesn't ask if she can walk with me. She assumes I want to be seen with her. Hilarious. She was in charge of the popular crowd in middle school, and lots of girls did stupid, humiliating things to make Anna like them.

That's not how I get things done. I didn't care then, and I don't care now. But—even though Anna would leave me behind in a heartbeat—it would be mean to leave her stranded in the hall when we're going to the same place.

Although I don't think it would kill her to learn how to read a map.

"When do you have lunch?" Anna asks.

"Fifth period," I say.

"Does Monica have fifth period lunch, too?" Anna asks.

I nod. "So does Chloe."

"Figures," Anna says. She looks disgusted. I'm starting to think her face really did freeze that way, like Monica and I used to joke it would. "I have one class with Carly and Karen. That's it! No homeroom, no lunch, and no study hall."

"That's too bad," I say.

It would be better for me if Anna and Carly were together. Then she wouldn't need me to show her around, and I wouldn't have to listen to her complain, and maybe then she'd actually stay away from Brad.

"And the school won't do anything about it!" Anna exclaims. "I asked them to change my schedule, but wanting to be with your best friend isn't a good enough reason."

"What a crybaby," someone says.

Anna and I pause to look back. Gina is behind us, walking with her entourage of cheerleaders.

"Poor little Anna misses her friends," Gina says in a mocking baby voice. Several people in the hall stop to stare. The other cheerleaders smirk and giggle. "Get over it and grow up," Gina tells Anna. "This is high school, not preschool."

Anna stiffens. I hold my breath. This is the third time I've heard Gina ridicule Anna. There's no way Anna will let it pass. The old Anna Dunlap is about to come out.

"Toddlers have better manners," Anna says with a nervous warble.

Several of the kids nearby burst out laughing. Then they move on.

Gina laughs, too, a short burst of anger. "Is that the best you've got?" she asks.

Anna turns to march away. "Let's go, Claudia."

I am totally amazed as I lead the way to our science class.

I don't think I've ever felt sorry for Anna Dunlap before.

"I hate high school!" Anna mutters through gritted teeth.

"It's the first day," I say. "Things will get better."

Anna smiles slightly. "What if they don't?"

"They always do," I say.

And I'm trying really hard to believe that. But if even Anna Dunlap can't survive . . .

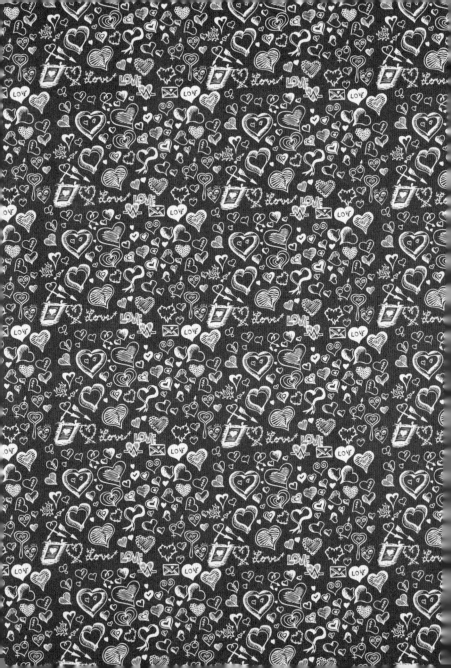

CHAPTER 4

Monica

It was weird that Claudia was wearing so much makeup. And it was really weird when she threw herself at Brad at the end of first period. But none of that compares to what happens when Chloe and I leave Mr. Harris's classroom: Claudia is walking away, talking to Anna.

"I can't believe this," I mutter.

"What's wrong?" Chloe asks.

"Nothing," I say. "Well, not nothing. I just think it's weird that Claudia's hanging out with Anna all of a sudden."

Chloe follows my gaze down the hall.

"Do you think she's jealous because now you have to split your best friend time between me and her?" Chloe asks.

I shrug. "I don't think so," I say. "We were best friends with Becca before she went to art school, and that wasn't ever weird."

"Then can't you be friends with me and Anna, too?" Chloe asks.

I almost laugh.

Then I remember that Chloe never had to deal with Anna in middle school.

Anna never spread rumors about Chloe wetting the bed or talking in her sleep about being in love with the principal. Anna didn't make fun of Chloe's clothes or keep her from going to all the good parties.

"I don't think I'll ever be friends with Anna Dunlap," I say. "You don't know her. She's not the kind of person I'm friends with."

"Okay," Chloe says. "Yikes."

"Anyway," I say, trying to lighten the mood. "Let's see if we can find our English class before we graduate."

Chloe and I make it to English on time. Even though Anna's BFFs Carly and Karen are both in our class, it goes by quickly.

For third period, I have Spanish. That classroom is in the opposite direction on the first floor.

I think.

I pull out my map to check. As I start toward the stairs, I see Rory walking toward me. He smiles and holds out his arms, like he's going to hug me.

I walk a little faster. I don't have much time, but I want to say hi.

"Rory!" a girl calls out.

Rory stops and looks back. "Hey, Gina. What's up?"

"I need a huge favor," Gina says. She moves up beside him, tilts her head, and smiles sweetly.

I hesitate. Does Rory know Gina is flirting?

Boys can be pretty dense about what girls do and why they do it sometimes.

"I'll help, if I can," Rory says.

"Are you busy after school?" Gina asks. She twirls some hair around her finger.

OMG.

It's so obvious that Gina likes Rory.

Not that I'm surprised. Lots of girls like him. How could they not? He's adorable, sweet, athletic, and smart. Still, Gina Tanner isn't just any girl. She's a cheerleader, and he's a football player, and they're both sophomores. And she's really, really pretty. If she weren't such a terrible person, I could see him liking her.

And now I'm wondering if he actually does, because he's walking with her. Rory glances over as he and Gina head around a corner.

"I've got to get to class!" he yells over to me. "See you later!"

"Okay!" I call back.

I feel awkward and a little dumb. I'm not even sure why, but I try to cover it, just in case anyone noticed. "See you later!"

I smile, but I'm not happy. So far today, two of my three best friends deserted me in the halls!

I hurry down the stairs, hoping I can get to room 135 before the bell rings.

* * *

Chloe and I are both famished after fourth period General Science. We don't have any trouble finding the cafeteria. You just have to follow the noise and the smell of French fries.

"Let's eat on the patio," Chloe says.

"Exactly what I was thinking," I say.

But all the picnic tables on the patio are taken. All the good tables in the cafeteria are full, too. The only ones left are the ones right by the garbage cans. Gross. That's just what I want on my first day of school. Lunch spent next to an overflowing garbage can.

Rory has lunch fifth period too, but I don't see him. I do spot Claudia sitting with some of my old friends. She waves us over.

Their table by the trash cans is noisy, but at least Anna isn't there. And Claudia seems happy to see me.

"How's it going so far, Monica?" Claudia asks. "It was weird not having any classes together this morning."

"Yeah, but we have homeroom and lunch," I say. "And algebra and study hall."

"That's the whole afternoon," Chloe says.

"True," Claudia says, nodding.

"Is anyone trying out for chorus?" Tommy asks.

"No way," I say. "I am as tone deaf as they come."

"I like to sing," Tommy says. "I don't really like auditioning. Drama club sounds better."

"Don't you have to audition for that?" Adam asks.

"Only for parts in the plays," Tommy explains. "I want to direct."

"Drama club is so popular, you might not get in until you're a junior," Chloe says. "Or at least that's what I heard."

"There's Brad!" Claudia exclaims softly.

"Brad!" someone calls out across the room. I spot Anna, sitting at the end of a table by herself.

Brad waves at Anna, but he walks toward us.

Claudia nudges me and points to the empty seat across from her. "Would you mind moving over there? Please."

I'm not thrilled about being pushed aside for a boy, but I do it anyway. As I stand up, one of the boys at the football table grabs Brad. Brad looks at Claudia, frowns, and then sits with the football team.

I sit back down.

"I wonder if that means Brad's going to make varsity," Adam says.

"It better," Claudia says.

She narrows her eyes, but she's not looking at Brad. She's watching Gina walk toward the football players.

I don't know why Claudia is mad at Gina. I'm just glad that Gina is with her friends and not with Rory.

The cheerleaders stop to talk to Anna. One of the girls knocks over her milk carton, and it spills on Anna's tray. I'm not positive, but I'm pretty sure it was deliberate.

"Wow, really?" I say. "Spilling milk? Who does that?"

Gina laughs as she and her friends walk away.

Anna jumps up and runs out. Claudia jumps up and runs after her.

I run after Claudia. I'm curious about why Claudia's suddenly spending so much time with Anna. We're supposed to be best friends, but she hasn't told me anything.

I follow them into the bathroom. Anna and

Claudia are standing by the sinks. Anna's crying. "Are you all right?" I ask.

"No!" Anna snaps. "Get out!"

"It might be better if you leave," Claudia says.

"Seriously?" I ask. But I'm not going to wait for an answer. Claudia's message is loud and clear.

Anna always gets what Anna wants. Anna wants Claudia there, but she doesn't want me, so I'm out.

Fine.

CHAPTER 5

CLAUDIA

When the phone rings on Monday night, I'm in the middle of a huge pile of homework. But I answer anyway, because it's Brad, and I'm so glad to hear his voice.

"Hey, cutie," he says.

I melt, of course.

Then I remember how he ditched me at lunch today, and I'm not as thrilled. "Hey," I say.

"Listen, I'm sorry about lunch," he says.

"Yeah, what happened?"

Brad sighs. "The football guys grabbed me. And I really wanted to sit with you, but I also really,

really want to make varsity. They're not posting the roster until Friday. I don't know if the other players have input. I had to sit with them. I figured if anyone would understand, it would be you. But when I saw the look on your face—"

He pauses, and then adds, "Are you mad?"

"No," I say. And it's true, I'm not. "I mean, it hurt my feelings, but I understand."

Brad exhales with relief. "Good," he says. "That's the last thing I want—to make you mad."

"You owe me lunch, though," I say, smiling.

I can hear his smile through the phone as he says, "As soon as the roster is posted? I'll never have lunch without you."

"Good," I say. "You better not. I'd miss you too much."

He sighs and says, "I'd miss you too."

* * *

Everyone's talking about the clubs when I get to my locker on Tuesday morning.

"All these clubs are for losers," Jenny says. "What did you pick?"

"Nothing, yet," I say. "I kind of want to write for the newspaper, but my dad said that Community Outreach would look better on college applications."

We start walking to class, and Monica does her imitation of my dad. "Claudia, journalism isn't going to get you into Harvard!"

I laugh. "It might. But he has a point about Community Outreach. It looks really good to admissions counselors at colleges."

"Well, we have to decide today," Jenny says.

"What about you?" I ask. "What did you pick?"

"I'm playing drums in the marching band," Jenny says. "But I haven't given up on girls' wrestling. Women wrestle on TV, so why can't girls wrestle at school?"

"Good question," I say.

In homeroom, I sit in an empty row. Monica starts to sit down next to me.

"Move over one," I say.

Monica frowns. "Why?"

I roll my eyes. "Chloe should sit there so Mr. Harris doesn't make us move."

"Why can't Chloe sit on your other side?" Monica asks.

"I'm saving that seat for Anna," I say.

"Oh, right. I forgot. Anna's your best friend now." Monica's eyes flash like shooting daggers.

What is up with her? "No, she's not," I say.

"It sure seems like it," Monica says. She sits down one seat over and opens her notebook, slamming it against the desk.

"Gina is trying to ruin Anna's first week of high school—" I begin.

"So?"

"So that's not cool," I say.

Chloe walks over and takes the seat between me and Monica. "What isn't cool?"

"How much Gina is picking on Anna," I say. "Anna only has one class with her old friends, Gina's picking on her, some cheerleader spilled her milk yesterday. I feel sorry for her."

"And freshmen have to stick together," Chloe adds.

"I guess so," Monica says.

I'm too busy the rest of the morning to worry about Anna or Monica. It's only the second day, but Ms. Marino gives us a pop quiz in science.

And then in third period, I have web design with Brad.

Web design is harder than I thought, but I'm going to try to stick with it. It would be so cool to be able to design websites. But I have to admit that part of why I'm taking the class is because Brad is in it.

He's seated at the end of a row when I walk in.

Adam is sitting beside him, but I go over anyway. They're playing an ancient game called Pong.

"Hi!" I say brightly. "Can I sit with you?"

"Of course," Brad says, staring at the screen and pushing keys. He doesn't look up, and Adam doesn't move over.

I stand behind them, watching a little white dot bounce back and forth across the screen until the game ends. Adam still doesn't move. But before I can ask him to move over, another boy starts to slide into the empty chair on Adam's other side.

"That's mine!" I say.

I grab the chair, but I don't sit down. I wait another agonizing minute. I keep thinking Brad will look up and say something, invite me to sit down, start a conversation. I don't know. Anything.

But the game has started again. Honestly, boys get into, like, a trance when they're playing video games.

And I'm not enough to shock him out of it.

* * *

In fourth period, I'm so focused on how to change my friendship with Brad into Claudia + Brad = true love that I almost forget to write down the English assignment. Between school stuff and Brad, I need a brain break by the time the bell rings for lunch.

Anna and I leave English and walk to the cafeteria together. We find an empty table, and when two senior girls sit at the other end, it doesn't matter. We still have four extra seats.

In a few minutes, Adam, Tommy, and Brad take three of them.

"Did anyone else sign up for drama club?" Tommy asks.

"I might," Anna says. "I'm a pretty good actress." She puts her hands on her heart and bats her eyes at Brad. "Oh, Romeo, Romeo. Where art thou, Romeo?"

Brad laughs. "Not bad."

My mouth falls open in shock. They're flirting right in front of me!

I have to do something.

But if I do something, Brad might think I'm being annoying or possessive.

But if I don't do anything, he might think I don't care!

But what's the right thing to do?

Tommy frowns. "Isn't it 'wherefore art thou'?" he asks.

Anna shrugs and rolls her eyes. "Whatever."

"What club did you pick, Claudia?" Brad asks, smiling at me. His foot brushes mine under the table.

"I'd love to be the ninth grade reporter for the Pine Creek Record," I say, finally deciding. "Even though my dad doesn't think it'd get me into Harvard."

"I heard that Vanessa already got that job," Adam says.

"That's perfect for her!" Anna exclaims. "Vanessa knows everything that's going on everywhere with everybody!" She smiles at Brad. "Right, Brad?" she asks, blinking.

Just then, Monica and Chloe walk up, carrying their trays.

"Do you guys have room for two more?" Monica asks, smiling.

"Not really," Anna says. Actually, there's one open seat and room for another chair. But before I can suggest it, Monica and Chloe walk away. Monica shoots us all a dirty look.

I think about going with them, but then Anna laughs at something Brad's saying.

No way am I leaving this table.

Monica knows how much I like Brad. And she knows that being in high school means things have changed.

I'm sure she'll understand why I want to stay here.

CHAPTER 6

Monica

I never expect Anna to be nice.

But I do expect Claudia to be. I expect her to stand up for me. I mean, she's standing up for Anna against Gina! Chloe and I get to lunch late, but there is plenty of room at Claudia's table. But when Anna says there isn't, Claudia doesn't do anything about it.

I don't know. I guess being friends with Little Miss Popular is more important than doing the right thing.

As Chloe and I push our way through the crowded cafeteria, my cheeks are burning. I just hope Claudia didn't notice. The best way to get back at her is to act like I don't care. Even if I do. Especially if I do.

"Let's sit over there," Chloe says. She points to a table that's half full of Rock Creek kids.

"At least one of us will fit in," I joke.

We don't ask. We just sit. Nobody tells us to leave. Finally, I feel like I can relax.

"Hey, beautiful!" Rory sits down next to me and flashes a brilliant smile. "This seat isn't taken, is it?" he asks, throwing his arm around my shoulder and giving me a squeeze.

"It is now," I say, beaming.

As soon as Rory's sitting there, the Rock Creek kids get real friendly real fast.

"Think you'll be on varsity this season, Rory?" a boy asks.

"Hope so," Rory answers. "I'll find out for sure when coach posts the roster on Friday." He smiles and adds, "But everyone's great."

"What position do you play?" one of the girls

asks. She gives Rory a wide-eyed stare. I can't help it—I roll my eyes. Rory's been playing football for years. If she were interested in football, she'd already know what position he plays.

"Wide receiver," Rory answers.

He doesn't seem annoyed or overly flattered by the attention. That's Rory. He just takes things as they come.

"What does a wide receiver do?" the other girl asks. She props her chin in her hand and tries to look interested.

I'm not fooled. They don't care about football. They're just trying to impress Rory.

"He catches the ball and makes touchdowns," I answer, bristling slightly. Rory's arm is still around me, but I nestle closer to him.

Inside, I have an OMG-what-did-I-just-do panic attack. If I act jealous every time a girl flirts which Rory—which seems like all girls, all the time—I might lose him as a friend. Not to mention destroy my chances of ever actually being his girlfriend.

"Yes," Rory says. "That's pretty much exactly what I do." He smiles and squeezes my shoulder, but then he lets his arm drop away from me.

"Aren't you from Pine Tree?" the boy asks me.

"I was," I say. "Now I'm from Pine Creek."

The boy sighs. "Yeah, we all are—like it or not."

"Do you think the rivalry is going to last?" I ask. "Between the two towns, I mean."

The boy shrugs. "Who knows?" he says.

Rory smiles at me. "It seems like it can't last," he says. "Now that we're all going to school together, seeing each other every day . . . what would be the point?" He moves his leg so that it's just barely touching mine, and a shiver runs up my spine.

Then I hear a familiar, unfriendly voice. "Rory!" It's Gina. She puts a hand on Rory's shoulder and hands him a little piece of paper. "That's my locker number. See you later!"

The Rock Creek girls hit Gina with hostile stares. She walks away, tossing her hair, and leaves.

I sigh. I can't compete with all the older, pretty girls who want to be Rory's girlfriend. I just remind myself that high school romances almost never last, but friends are forever.

As long as they aren't fair-weather friends like Claudia.

Claudia and Anna have sixth period algebra with Chloe and me, but they don't wait for us to walk to class after lunch. They don't save us seats and they don't walk with us after class, either. Not that I care.

Chloe leaves for an appointment seventh period. I head to study hall alone. I keep an eye out for Claudia and Anna so I can avoid them.

I can't avoid Gina Tanner.

Gina bumps into me and makes me drop my backpack. A flap flips open and all my pens and pencils roll out.

I'm sure she did it on purpose.

"Why don't you watch where you're going?" Gina snaps.

"Why don't you?" I snap back as I stoop to pick up my things.

"Aren't you going to apologize for running into me?" Gina asks.

"I would if I did, but I didn't, so no," I say. "Don't you have a class?"

"Just watch it." Gina walks away in a huff.

The run-in makes me wonder. Maybe Gina hates all ninth-grade girls, not just Anna.

* * *

After school, things go from bad to worse.

I see Rory standing with Gina by her locker. She's talking, and he's hanging on to every word.

Getting ignored by one of my best friends is enough rejection for one day. I won't risk it again. I pretend I don't see them and keep walking.

"Hey, Monica!" Rory calls out. I stop, and he walks over. "How was your day?" he asks.

I shrug. "It was okay," I say.

"I'm taking Gina home. Do you want a ride? It's on my way."

"Not today, thanks," I say. If Gina says something rude, I might say something I'll regret— especially if Rory and Gina have something going.

I don't want to look like a lovesick moron. So I lie. "I'm, uh—meeting someone on the bus."

"Oh. Well, okay. I'll see you later." Rory hurries back to Gina.

I stomp down the hall. I can't get away fast enough.

That's when I make a decision. I am not going to drive myself crazy wanting someone I can't have. I take a deep breath, but my heart flip-flops when I hear my name again.

It's Brad.

"Can I ask you something?" he asks. Brad looks as unhappy as I feel.

"Sure," I say. "What's going on?"

"Maybe you can tell me," Brad says. "Why is Claudia acting so weird?"

She took a make-me-popular pill and turned into a major jerk, I think.

"Weird in what way?" I ask.

"Well, she's been kind of clingy, for one thing." Brad exhales in frustration. "I've got a lot to worry about right now with football and classes and everything. I want Claudia to be Claudia! The Claudia I can count on. Normal Claudia, you know? I don't want her to be Weird Flaky Freak Claudia."

"What else is she doing that's not normal?" I ask.

Brad shrugs. "She looks weird in all that makeup."

I resist the urge to agree. And I don't tell him Claudia has been weird with me, too. I don't want it to be my fault if Brad breaks things off with her. He has to settle his Claudia problem on his own.

But I'm on his side on this one.

"It's the first week of high school. Everything's a little weird. I mean, what's with Rory and Gina?" As soon as I blurt out the question, I gasp.

I did not mean to ask that!

"I don't know," Brad says. "It's kind of weird. I always thought Gina was horrible, but a bunch of the guys on the team think she's the hottest cheerleader."

Great.

Brad checks the time on his phone and sighs. "I gotta run," he says. "Practice."

"See you," I say.

I get on the bus and drop into a seat with a heavy sigh. So far, high school isn't anything like I thought it would be.

Except for Chloe, I feel like everyone hates me. Like I'm an outcast.

"Can I sit here?" a boy asks, sitting down next to me. "I'm Austin Harper," he adds.

I look over and grin. Austin isn't as gorgeous as Rory, but he's cute! And he has a nice smile.

"I'm Monica Murray," I say. "And of course you can sit there. Are you new here?"

"Sort of," Austin says. "I used to go to Rock Creek but then we moved to Pine Tree. It's all the same now, I guess. Do you like movies?"

"I love movies," I say. "I saw Star Pirates last weekend—"

"Star Pirates was fantastic!" Austin exclaims. "I thought for sure they'd mess it up, but they didn't. The story was totally true to the comic. What did you think?"

"It was pretty good for an action—"

Austin interrupts me again. "I gave it five stars on my blog. It's called Austin Prime, if you want to look it up later. I get a hundred hits a week!"

Austin talks, and I listen, until he gets off the bus. I'm not bored. I'm not really paying attention, though.

I'm thinking that a new boyfriend might be just what I need.

And Austin Harper is perfect!

CHAPTER 7

CLAUDIA

I wanted to talk to Monica after school, but one minute she was at her locker and the next minute she was gone! She didn't even say goodbye.

She didn't answer my texts or pick up when I called.

Monica won't speak to me, and I don't know why!

But I'm going to find out.

Monica's grandpa opens the door when I ring the bell. He lets me in and smiles. I guess Monica didn't tell him she's upset.

"Hi, Claudia," her grandpa says. "Monica's in her room."

"Thanks." I hurry down the hall and burst through Monica's door. She looks up from her notebook. "Are you mad at me?" I ask—quick, before she can kick me out. Monica squints, folds her arms, and sets her jaw. She's mad, all right!

"What did I do?" I ask.

Monica glares at me. "Anna made Chloe and me feel like total losers at lunch! And you didn't say a single word!"

I am so shocked, all I can do is stare back at her. I had no idea.

"You could have made more room for us at the table," Monica said.

"I know," I admit. "I didn't mean to make you feel bad. I almost got up and came with you!"

"But you didn't," Monica says.

"I wanted to sit with Brad," I explain. "I thought you'd understand."

"I wouldn't ditch you to sit with Austin," Monica mutters.

"Wait a second. Who's Austin?" I ask. "I thought you liked Rory."

"I do," Monica says, "as a friend. Rory is popular and good-looking and a sports star and he's a sophomore! It's obviously never going to work. I don't want a broken heart or a broken friendship."

Rory always seems happy when he's with Monica. In fact, I have always assumed they'd end up together.

"I'm pretty sure that wouldn't happen," I say. "Rory wouldn't break your heart."

"Unless he's going out with someone else," Monica says. Then she winces, like she shouldn't have said anything.

"Who is he going out with?" I ask.

This is the kind of stuff best friends always tell each other, but Monica hasn't even dropped a hint! I guess she's more upset than I realized.

"It doesn't matter," Monica says with a shrug. "I met someone else."

"Austin?" I ask, sitting on the edge of the bed. I notice that Monica still has framed horse show photos and ribbons hanging on the walls, but her unicorn posters are gone.

"Austin sat with me on the bus," Monica says. "He asked for my phone number before he got off."

"Did he call?" I ask. I'm mostly relieved that Monica is talking to me again.

"My cell phone rang before I got in the door!" Monica exclaims. "He's very cute and very cool. He used to go to Rock Creek but his family moved over the county line this summer. He writes a blog called Austin Prime. It's mostly about movies and books and comics, but he loves video games, too. Anything that's science fiction or fantasy."

I nod, but it's hard to concentrate on Austin. I'm worried about Brad. It seems like he flirts with everyone but me!

"Anyway, he wants a game called *Castle Troll*,"

Monica continues. "It's so rare he can't even find it online! I told him your brother might have it or know someone who does."

"I'll ask Jimmy," I say. Then I quickly change the subject. "I know Brad likes me, but he doesn't always treat me like a girl. It really bothers me."

Monica looks puzzled. "I thought you liked that about him."

"I did," I say, "when we were still kids. I love being Brad's friend, but that's not enough anymore. I want to be his girlfriend."

Monica frowns, but she doesn't say anything. So I keep talking. "I know it's all super tense now, but sooner or later we'll make friends with the Rock Creek kids—like Brad and that Tyler guy on the football team. But what if Brad meets a girl he likes better than me? Like you met Austin?"

Monica hesitates, then exhales. "Can I be honest?" She asks.

"Of course," I say.

"Well, the heavy makeup makes you look—" Monica hesitates.

"Too old?" I guess.

"Too something," Monica says.

"Okay," I say slowly. I don't agree, but that's okay.

"And making new friends doesn't mean you'll lose your old friends," Monica says. Then she adds, "Unless you ignore them."

I'm positive she's talking about Anna. I'm not trying to replace Monica, but before I can explain— again—she has one more thing to say.

"Or start getting clingy like you're doing with Brad," Monica says. "If you don't cool it, you could lose him."

Okay. Now I'm mad! Monica is being mean to get back at me for brushing her off at lunch.

"Why would you say that?" I ask stiffly.

Monica sighs. "That's what Brad told me."

I don't believe her.

· CLAUDIA ·

CHAPTER 8:

Monica

Austin doesn't get on the bus Wednesday morning, so I send him a text.

Are you sick?

Not too flirtatious, but it's not too bold, either—just in case he doesn't like me as much as it seems. I'm not sure how I feel about him, I guess. So playing it cool is playing it smart. I don't want to mess it up like Claudia's messing up everything with Brad.

Claudia was upset last night when I told her what Brad said. She didn't really believe me. And she wasn't exactly thrilled with my honesty. But I don't know why she's mad at me.

I was trying to help.

I'm pretty sure Brad likes her as much as she likes him. But if the real Claudia doesn't show up soon, he might find someone else.

She should have listened to me.

Austin sends me a text right before we get to school.

Missed bus. Mom driving me. See you there!

All my friends—and my maybe-she-is-maybe-she-isn't-former-best friend--are in homeroom when I get there. Claudia is sitting between Brad and Anna. I sit with Chloe. She saved me a seat. Austin dashes in right before the bell.

"Hey, Monica!" Austin says, grinning. He grabs a seat in the front of the room.

"How do you know Austin Harper?" Chloe asks.

"I met him on the bus yesterday," I say.

"Oh," Chloe says.

I'm dying to tell Chloe everything, and it seems like she wants to tell me something too, but the bell rings. We can't talk on the way to second period, either. Austin is in our English class, and he wants to walk with us.

"So, Austin, I might have a lead on that game you want," I say.

"Castle Troll?" Austin asks. "Really?"

"Maybe," I say. "I know someone who knows someone."

"Great!" Austin exclaims. "They should have done a *Castle Troll II* or at least kept making the first one, but they didn't so it's almost impossible to find. I guess they thought *Castle Wars* would be enough to replace it."

"That's interesting," I say. Actually, it isn't, but I don't want to hurt Austin's feelings. "What are you doing this weekend?"

"Watching a science fiction movie marathon on

the Sci-Fi & Fantasy Channel," Austin says. "It's on from midnight Friday until noon Sunday. I've got the DVR cleared and ready to go."

Then he starts going into detail about every. Single. Movie. Every one that he's going to watch all weekend. When he's going to take breaks to nap, when—and what—he'll eat. I try twice to change the subject, but Austin is still talking about the marathon when we walk into room 209.

"I might even do a live commentary on my blog," Austin says.

I sit between Chloe and Austin in English. Chloe looks disturbed, but we can't talk because Austin is still blabbing about the stupid movie marathon.

Then we don't get a chance to talk until fourth period science, when we're in the same class again. As soon as I walk in, I see Chloe tensing up.

"What's bothering you, Chloe?" I ask.

"Austin obviously likes you," Chloe says. "But if you like Rory, it's not fair to string Austin along."

I hadn't thought of it like that. Chloe is being honest, just like I was last night, but I don't get mad like Claudia did.

"Rory and I are still friends," I say. "I just don't want to get between him and Gina."

As soon as I say the words, fireworks go off in my brain. Now I know why I didn't tell Claudia about Gina last night: Saying something out loud makes it feel real.

"What?" Chloe looks stunned and lowers her voice. "What makes you think Rory is going out with Gina?"

"They walk to class together and meet after school, and Rory drives Gina home. That's hanging out."

"But hanging out and going out aren't the same thing," Chloe says. "Besides, you and Rory are best friends. He'd tell you if he was dating someone."

I shrug. "I didn't ask."

Chloe fixes me with a hard stare. "Why not?"

"Well, because—" I pause, and then spit out the words. "If Rory tells me he likes Gina, I can't even daydream about being his girlfriend anymore."

"So you do like Rory!" Chloe exclaims. "Aha! I knew it."

I can't deny it. I just sigh.

"What are you going to do?" Chloe asks.

I honestly don't know.

* * *

When I walk into the cafeteria at lunchtime, Claudia, Anna, Adam, and Brad do not wave me over.

I wonder if Claudia and I will ever make up.

Then I see Rory, and I feel worse. He's sitting at the football table with Gina, some players, and another cheerleader.

Wonderful.

Chloe is already sitting with Tommy. I take a step toward them, but then stop. I can't let Gina make me too scared to talk to one of my best friends. I know Gina likes Rory, but what if he doesn't like her? What if he's just being nice like Brad? I walk over.

"Hi, Rory," I say. Everyone looks at me, and I realize I don't have anything else to say! I just blurt out, "Have you got a minute?"

"No, I don't," Rory says. "Not right now."

Gina smiles and turns so her shoulder is touching Rory. He doesn't flinch.

"Maybe later," I say. I leave quickly, before I make a bigger fool of myself. I sit with Chloe and Tommy and save a seat for Austin.

Tommy is scowling at his sandwich.

"What's wrong, Tommy?" I ask.

"I missed the auditions for chorus," Tommy explains.

"I thought you weren't going to try out," I say.

"I changed my mind," Tommy says. "But I didn't check for the audition times on the bulletin board in homeroom."

"The gaming club is first come first served," Austin says, putting his tray on the table and sitting down next to me. "After the juniors and seniors sign up, there aren't many slots left. I hope I get in."

My mind wanders as Austin babbles about the gaming club. I've never had boy trouble before, but I do now!

Austin is cute and nice, but he talks a lot. And he's never once asked me about myself.

Rory is gorgeous and sweet, but he just brushed me off. Did he have a good reason? Is there a good reason? I can't ask if Rory doesn't have time to talk to me.

Austin likes me, but I'm not sure I want to be his girlfriend. I've only known him one day.

When you don't know what to do, sometimes the best thing to do is nothing.

When I tune back into the conversation, Austin is still talking. "I don't know why the school banned *Saga*," he says. "It's not nearly as violent as some games."

Normally, Tommy spends all of lunch telling jokes. Today, he's too bummed about chorus to interrupt Austin.

Chloe stares at me. I can tell she wants me to get Austin to shut up. But I don't know how.

"Newspaper critics don't look at movies the same way kids do," Austin says. "That's why I started my blog. So people our age can get my opinion. It's called Austin Prime if you want to look it up—"

Does Austin know he hogs the conversation? If he doesn't figure it out, nobody will want to be around him—or me!

Jenny Pinski sits down just as Austin starts talking about the movie marathon. Again.

"Half the movies in the marathon are in black

and white," Austin says. "I've never seen *Forsaken Planet*. They say it's awful, but I can't wait—"

"I can't wait for you to shut up," Jenny says.

Austin wince-smiles. "Sorry about that."

"Whatever," Jenny says. She turns to the rest of us and says, "I finally talked to Coach about girls' wrestling."

When Jenny Pinski talks, we all listen, whether we want to or not. We've been doing it for years so it's a habit. This time, everyone really is interested in her efforts to start a girls' wrestling team.

"So?" I ask, thrilled to be able to change the subject. "What did he say?"

Jenny shrugs. "Coach said the school board might okay an exhibition team—if I can find three other girls to sign up!"

"I might know someone," Austin says.

We spend the rest of our lunch period listening to Jenny and Austin talk about wrestling.

I didn't know the Sci-Fi and Fantasy Channel shows wrestling two nights a week.

And frankly? I didn't care.

CHAPTER 9

CLAUDIA

I'm glad Monica isn't at her locker on Thursday morning. I'm still mad, and she's not speaking to me! We avoided each other all day yesterday. It feels awful—like burgers without fries, Christmas without presents, or a phone without unlimited texting.

Anna isn't here, either, but that's actually kind of a relief. She's like a permanent accessory! I don't want to cut her loose, but I wish she'd give me a little space.

I am glad to see Brad walking down the hall. "Hey, Brad!" I yell. I expect him to smile and rush up like he always does. Instead, he turns around.

My mind reels as I watch him walk away.

When did Brad start avoiding me?

Was Monica right?

Have I been so afraid of losing Brad that I've driven him away?

Nothing else explains what just happened. Somehow, I've got to fix it.

I rush to homeroom and sit in the desk behind Brad. Tyler and Adam are in the seats beside him. They're talking about the football roster that's coming out tomorrow. "I don't have a chance of making first string," Tyler says.

Suddenly, I know why Brad isn't talking to me! He's stressed about his position on the team, and I haven't been there for him. Some best friend I turned out to be.

"I practiced my kick all summer," Adam says, "but I'm still not good enough to start."

"Brad is," I say. I smile when he looks back. "You were the best quarterback in three counties."

"Tell me about it!" Tyler exclaims. "I had to play against him."

"If you don't make first string now, you will before the season ends," I say.

"Think so?" Brad asks.

"No doubt," I say. I want Brad to know that I believe in him.

We talk football until the bell rings. Right now I don't know if Brad and I are still on track to be a real couple, but at least we're still friends. That's the part that matters the most.

Next I have to set things right with Monica. Except for first period American History, we don't have any morning classes together. I plan to talk to her at lunch, but Anna sees Carly laughing with Gina and has a nervous breakdown in the hall.

"Gina is being nice to Carly to torture me," Anna says as we duck into the restroom. "She's trying to ruin my life!"

Anna isn't wrong. Gina picks on other freshmen,

but she's a hundred times meaner to Anna. I just don't know why.

Monica and I both have sixth period algebra, but Austin Harper sits next to her. Anna and I sit behind them two rows back. I hear Austin and Monica talking.

"When will your friend know about Castle Troll?" Austin asks.

"I don't know," Monica says.

Oops! I forgot to ask Jimmy about the game! Shoot.

"I hope you find out soon," Austin says. He keeps talking after the bell rings. "The perks for players who've gotten through the top levels are unbelievable."

"Settle down, class," Mr. Palmira says.

Austin leans closer to Monica and lowers his voice. "Extra game money and enhanced powers don't matter much if you're just playing yourself on a computer, but it makes a huge difference when you're playing with hundreds of other people online."

"I'll ask her tonight," Monica whispers.

"End that conversation now," the teacher snaps, "or both of you will be in detention today."

Austin stops talking. He doesn't seem bothered by the public rebuke.

I can't see Monica's face, but I know she's mortified. She hates getting into trouble.

Normally Monica and I have the same seventh period study hall. Today I have a Community Outreach meeting in the library. All the members are expected to work on the club's projects.

I look for Monica when I go to my locker. She's not there, but Gina ambushes Anna and me.

"Dressing like a *Teen Life* model doesn't cut it with the cool crowd in high school," Gina tells Anna. "Here, in high school, you actually have to be cool to be popular."

I shrivel inside.

I expect Anna to fall apart, and I don't want to spend the next hour putting her back together again. It's getting old.

Instead, she stands up for me!

"Fashion always counts," Anna says, glaring at Gina. "And Claudia is one of the cool kids."

"Get real," Gina scoffs and walks away.

"What is her problem?" Anna asks.

"I have a theory," I say. I've been thinking about it since lunch. "Maybe Gina likes a sophomore boy that likes you, and she's jealous."

"Seriously?" Anna perks up.

"I'm just guessing," I say. "But my brother is older and he dates younger girls."

"A secret admirer!" Anna exclaims, grinning. "That would be fantastic! Especially if Gina just hates me because she's jealous!"

After Anna leaves, Monica walks over.

"Can I talk to you for a minute?" she asks.

"Yes!" I say. Before I can tell her how I wish I hadn't ignored her advice about Brad, she trashes my theory about Gina.

"Gina doesn't like someone that likes Anna," Monica says. "Gina likes Rory."

"No way!" I exclaim. "But Rory doesn't like her back, does he?"

"I hope not," Monica says with a sigh. "I haven't worked up the nerve to ask."

I'm pretty sure Monica just likes the attention from Austin. Her heart belongs to Rory.

"You have to ask him," I say. "I acted all weird because I thought Brad was flirting when he was just being nice like he always is."

"Did you talk to Brad?" Monica asks.

"Yes, he's worried about football," I say. "I think we're okay now. Thanks for the heads up."

"I'm glad it helped," Monica says.

"I wish you could help me figure out why Gina is so down on Anna," I say.

"That's easy," Monica says. "Gina hated Anna in middle school because Anna was a year younger but she had more power. Gina couldn't do anything about it back then without getting into trouble. But everyone expects the older kids to give ninth graders a hard time."

Monica's theory makes sense. Gina is a sophomore cheerleader. She has power, and she doesn't want Anna Dunlap, the dreaded and—don't ask me why—adored leader of Pine Tree Middle School, to move in and take over.

"If Gina is afraid of Anna, doesn't that mean Anna still has power?" I ask.

"It would," Monica says, "but Anna doesn't have homeroom or lunch with her old friends. So she's like a general without an army."

"That's why I started hanging out with her," I say. "I felt bad for her."

Monica sighs. "I'm sorry I was jealous. I know it was stupid, but I just didn't get it. Anna never did anything for us unless she wanted something."

"I'm sorry I didn't try harder to include you and Chloe," I say. "I've missed you."

"Me, too," Monica says, smiling.

I feel like twenty tons of bricks suddenly slid off my shoulders! Monica and I are still best friends, and I won't do anything to ruin it again.

I hope Anna understands, but I'm not counting on it.

CHAPTER 10

Monica

I can't wait to see Claudia on Friday morning. Chloe and I save a seat for her in homeroom, but she's late. I block Austin when he tries to take it.

"Sorry, but I have to talk to Chloe," I say. "In private."

"Oh, okay." Austin looks surprised, but he shrugs and finds another seat.

I don't feel guilty. I'm still upset. I almost got detention yesterday because Austin wouldn't stop shut up.

I have to talk to him about it. I just don't want to do it right now.

"Is everything still patched up between you and Claudia?" Chloe asks.

"Yes, but that's not what I wanted to tell you," I say.

"Did you talk to Rory?" Chloe's eyes light up.

I shake my head. "I called him last night, but he was asleep and his mom wouldn't wake him up."

"There's a big horse show in next month," Chloe says. "He's been working extra hours at the barn plus football and school."

"Right," I say. I don't tell her I also sent Rory a text this morning.

Hey, Rory! Let's talk. Call me.

I haven't heard back, but that doesn't change how I feel.

"I thought about what you said," I tell Chloe. "I don't want to be Austin's girlfriend, and it's not fair to let him think I do."

"Did you tell him?" Chloe asks.

"Not yet, but I will," I assure her.

"Good," Chloe says. "And for the record, I don't believe Rory would go out with a bully like Gina. But if they are dating—it won't last."

I'm ready to wait. No matter how long it takes.

* * *

At lunch, Chloe and I join Austin and Tommy. They're sitting at the same table we've had all week—by the trash cans. Nobody else wants it, but that's okay. We don't have to fight to save seats for our friends.

There's an empty chair right next to Austin, but I hesitate before sitting down in it. If I sit next to him, I know he'll think that I'm still interested. If I don't sit next to him, he'll know something is wrong, and I don't want to explain until I can do it in private. So I sit next to him.

I wave when Claudia and Anna come in. Claudia

waves back, but after they talk for a minute, Anna leaves. I have an instant she-is-such-a-jerk reaction. Anna ignored or made fun of us in middle school, and it sure looks like she doesn't want to sit with us now.

I'm annoyed, but I don't say anything when Claudia joins the table.

"Have you seen Brad?" Claudia asks.

"Not since second period," I say. I haven't seen Rory, either. None of the players are sitting at the team table.

"Where did Anna go?" Chloe asks.

"She went to see if she made it into the drama club," Claudia says.

I'm not convinced that's the real reason Anna left. She's had Claudia to herself all week. She's probably not happy that we're best friends again.

"They just posted the club lists," Claudia adds.

"Chorus, too?" Chloe asks.

"Did you try out?" I ask. Auditioning is huge, and Chloe never said a word!

"Yeah," Chloe admits. "Auditions were seventh period on Tuesday. I wasn't going to tell you until I knew if I made it or not." She laughs. "Too late now, I guess!"

"Anna wanted me to sign up for drama club with her," Claudia says. "But I'm not into acting, so why take a slot that someone else really —"

Austin interrupts. "The gaming club list must be up, too. I want to know, but I don't want to know, you know? In case I didn't get in. I've talked to twenty other guys that signed up, so it's a long shot —"

"I want to know now," Tommy says. He leaves so fast I wonder if he just wants to get away from Austin.

"Hey!" Jenny yells from the middle of the cafeteria. She stands on a chair and waves a piece of paper. "I'm posting the sign-up sheet for the girls' exhibition wrestling team in the gym! We've got four counting me, but there's room for more!"

Chloe jumps up. "I can't stand the suspense about chorus!" she says. "I have to find out if I made it. See you guys later."

After Chloe runs out, I whisper to Claudia. "I need to talk to Austin—alone."

Claudia whispers back, "Gotcha." She doesn't bother making up an excuse. She just leaves.

And the moment I've been dreading is here.

"I have something to tell you, Austin," I say. "And I hope you don't take it the wrong way."

Austin frowns. "What?"

"Well, two things, actually." I take a breath and go for it. "I like you, but just as a friend, and my friends like you, too, but you have to give other people a chance to talk or—well, nobody will want to be around you."

"Oh." Austin nods. Then he stands up. "I think I'll go check the club lists too."

I feel horrible, partly because I'm so relieved.

My phone beeps and my heart skips a beat. I have a text message from Rory.

Casey's Café 7:00?

I hope the message means what I think it means. I'll know tonight, when I meet Rory at the coffee house.

CHAPTER 11

CLAUDIA

The aroma of coffee and cinnamon tickles my nose when I walk into Casey's Cafe after school. My mouth waters. I love Casey's chocochinos! Every time I come here, that's what I order.

The coffeehouse isn't fancy. The decor is thrift store hand-me-down, but that's a major plus—it's comfortable, and when we're there, we just want to hang out and talk. The tables, chairs, and sofas are scratched, lumpy, and don't match, but the prices are good and the menu is fantastic.

I'm not the first to arrive. Monica and Chloe

are sitting with Brad and Tommy. They've already pulled two tables together. I told Anna I'd wait for her, so I don't go over right away.

Casey keeps two racks full of magazines and newspapers for his customers. Tommy is reading something aloud from the Harmon County Herald. It must be funny because everyone laughs.

Even Monica. She was disappointed when I told her that we were all meeting at the coffee house tonight. Our first week of high school is over and the football roster was posted, so there's a lot to talk about.

Brad and Adam didn't make varsity, but Brad is the #3 quarterback behind two seniors! Rory is the starting wide receiver. Yay, team!

Monica thought Rory just wanted to see her. He'd sent her a text, or something.

I told her that's why he sent her a text, to make sure she'd be here.

I could tell she wanted to believe me, but she's scared. This thing with Rory has been building for a long time, and Monica's still not convinced he feels the same way about her. If she gets her hopes up and then it turns out that she's right about Gina, the heartbreak will be worse.

I don't know what to think when Gina Tanner walks in with two other cheerleaders. She doesn't speak to me. She just gives me a sidelong look of loathing as she walks by.

I make a mental note: Do not be a conceited creep when I'm a sophomore.

"What are we doing here?" one of Gina's friends asks.

"I told you," Gina says. "I heard Rory and some other guys on the team talking after school. They were making plans for tonight. He's going to be here."

"Why do we have to suffer because you're in love?" the first girl asks with a pout. "I thought you found out that he has a girlfriend. That Monica girl."

I grin.

"Shut up," Gina says. She leads them to a table by the front window.

Monica frowns when she sees the girl who's trying to steal the love of her life. She doesn't know what I just found out! I can't wait to tell her—after Anna arrives.

When the bell over the front door rings again, I look over. Anna walks in. Just as she spots me, Carly jumps out of a cracked leather booth. She was obviously waiting for Anna.

"Surprise!" Carly squeals. "You are not going to believe what happened!"

"What?" Anna asks. She's all smiles.

"I got into chorus!" Carly says. "So that means they had to change my schedule!"

Anna gasps. "You mean—"

"Starting Monday we'll be together for homeroom and fifth period lunch!" Carly exclaims. "Plus, I'm not sure how many classes we have together, but I know it's more than one."

"That is so great!" Anna hugs Carly. Then Carly pulls her into the ladies' room.

Anna doesn't give me another glance. I wait for a minute, but she doesn't pop out to invite me into their cozy circle.

I'm sort of stunned when I realize my feelings are hurt. I actually started to like Anna this week. Of course, she needed me, but still—I didn't think she'd dump me the minute Carly came back.

"Claudia!" Brad calls out my name and pats the empty chair beside him. I put Anna out of my mind and hurry over with a smile on my face.

"I was starting to worry you weren't coming," Brad says.

"I couldn't wait to get here," I say.

I slide into the seat next to him, and he reaches over and squeezes my knee.

"And not just because of the coffee chocochinos, either," Monica teases.

Chloe giggles and Tommy rolls his eyes.

I blush a little, but that's okay. I'm sad about Anna, but Monica and I are still best friends forever and Brad wants to be with me. I feel a little silly for thinking everything would be different when we started high school. But nothing important has changed—except one thing.

Brad reaches for my hand under the table.

· CLAUDIA ·

CHAPTER 12

Monica

When I get to Casey's, everything is perfect until Gina walks in with two other girls.

After I got Rory's text, I thought I might be the girl—the one he wants for a girlfriend. We've been close friends for two years, but like Chloe said, "Hanging out isn't the same as going out."

What's really strange is that it wasn't the idea of Rory and Gina together that finally made me realize that I like him. A lot.

It was Austin!

Being with Austin didn't make my skin tingle

or my heart race or take my breath away. That only happens when I'm with Rory.

The hard, cold fact of the matter is I'll be devastated if Rory likes Gina. Devastated.

But I don't know that he likes her—not for sure—and I don't want to spoil the First Week of High School Survival Party for everyone else. I crack a joke when Claudia sits down and tells Brad that she wouldn't miss a night out at Casey's.

"And it's not just because of the coffee chocochinos, either," I tease.

Every time we had coffee somewhere else this summer, she'd tell me it wasn't as good as Casey's chocochino. But I also happen to know that she'd drink the worst coffee in the world if it was in a mug on a table near Brad. It's pretty sweet, how much they like each other.

Claudia rolls her eyes, but she smiles too. At least that's going right!

"Are you psyched because you got into drama club?" Chloe asks Tommy.

"I'm mad with glee!" Tommy weirds out for five seconds, making faces and shaking his head and hands. Then he gets more serious and adds, "It should be cool, even if they don't let me direct until I'm a senior."

Funny. A year ago, Tommy wouldn't have gotten serious at all. He would've just kept being weird old class clown Tommy. I guess we really are starting to be different.

That's when Claudia leans toward me and whispers in my ear. "There's something you should know about—"

"Gina?" I whisper. My throat tightens and my stomach hurts.

"Yes! I know for a fact that—"

My phone beeps. I have a text message. "Is that from Rory?" Claudia asks as I'm reading it.

"No, it's from Austin," I say. "I guess he's here. He wants me to meet him outside."

"Okay, but first—" Claudia says.

I cut her off. "I'll be right back."

I hurry out, grateful for the distraction. Good or bad, whatever Claudia wants to tell me will still be good or bad news when I get back.

Austin is pacing on the sidewalk in front of the café. When he sees me, he sighs.

"I'm sorry if you hate me," I say, "but I had—"

"I don't hate you!" Austin exclaims. "I want to thank you."

"For what?" I ask, puzzled.

"For being a good enough friend to be honest with me," he says. "That took a lot of guts."

I'm not sure what to say. No problem. Austin keeps talking. "I know I talk too much," he goes on. "I just get so excited about stuff I get carried away. See? I'm doing it right now! And then nobody wants to talk to me or be friends with me or—"

"How did you know where to find me?" I ask.

"Tommy told me," Austin says.

"Well, it sounds like nobody's stopped talking to

you, then," I point out. "It's going to be fine, Austin. Seriously. I promise."

"As long as I shut off the motor mouth," Austin says.

"Or put it in idle now and then," I joke. "I can kick you under the table, if you think it will help."

He smiles at me. "Why not? It works for Jenny! Is she coming tonight?"

"I don't know," I say. I'm pretty sure nobody in our group invited Jenny. But the way Austin asked makes me think he likes her! Jenny is a science fiction fan and video game player, too.

"Are you coming in?" I ask as I turn to go inside.

"Right behind you," Austin says. He types a text as we walk.

So two of my three people problems are fixed. Claudia is still my best friend, and Austin doesn't hate me.

I hope the third one works out, too. That's an all or nothing deal. I try to think about what I'll do if it turns out he and Gina are a real-life love affair. I picture myself never talking to him again, but it just makes me feel empty and sad inside.

I can't imagine not having Rory in my life.

So if he and Gina get together, I know I'll still be friends with him—even though I'd hate every single second he spent with Gina.

But Gina would never let Rory be friends with another girl.

When Austin and I walk back to the table, everyone starts laughing. I look back and laugh, too. Austin has a big piece of tape over his mouth. He rips it off. "Hey, everyone. I can take a hint!" Austin says. Then he sits down and just smiles.

Rory is late. I check my phone. There's no message.

"Anna's here," Chloe says.

"Really?" Claudia says. She looks surprised when Anna and Carly walk up to the table.

"Is there room for two more?" Anna asks.

"You want to sit with us?" I ask. I don't mean to be rude. I'm just stunned, and it slips out.

"Well, I could use a fun night among friends," Anna says shyly. She looks at Claudia and smiles. "Especially the ones who saved me from total insanity this week."

"Claudia was so nice to Anna all week," Carly says, "and that makes her a friend of mine."

"And all her friends, too," Anna adds. "Unless you guys don't—"

"We've got room," Claudia says. She breaks into a huge grin. "But don't sit next to Monica. That seat's saved."

I cross my fingers. Rory always sits with us, but that was before Rock Creek and Pine Tree combined into one school and Gina Tanner met him.

"This one is saved, too," Austin says. He puts his arm on the back of the empty chair beside him.

"Who else is coming besides Rory?" Chloe asks.

"Jenny," Austin says. "I just texted her and told

her to meet me here, but we won't stay very long. We're going to watch the science fiction movie marathon tonight at her house."

"Is she getting that girls' wrestling team going?" Brad asks.

Austin smiles. "Yeah," he says. "Turns out there are actually a bunch of girls who want to do it. And she did some more research and found out that there are a few other teams in the conference, so it sounds like they'll get to compete for real this year."

They keep talking about wrestling and clubs and homework and teachers, but I tune out. Until I hear the bell above the door jingle as the door opens.

Rory walks in. All six feet of him. Every time I see him, it's like I forgot how adorable he is until that exact moment. The butterflies in my stomach come back. He pauses to look around and smiles broadly when our eyes meet. He doesn't even notice Gina sitting by the front window. He heads straight for our table and sits down beside me.

"Sorry I'm late," Rory says, squeezing my

shoulder. "I'm glad you could come. And I hope it's okay that it's not just us. I figured we all needed some good old-fashioned hanging-out time, and you and I can have plenty of alone time now that tryouts are over."

"Of course," I say, smiling up at him.

"Rory!" Gina calls out.

Rory glances back. "Hey, Gina." He gives her a half-hearted wave.

"Come over here!" she says, patting the seat next to her.

"I'm here with Monica," Rory tells her, and turns back to me, rolling his eyes as he turns away. "I gave Gina a few rides because her car broke down, so now she thinks she owns me," he mutters.

"Girls can be like that," I say.

"You're not." Rory smiles. "I'm sorry I've been so busy. Believe me, I'd rather eat lunch with you than huddle with the team. Now that the roster is out, the pressure is off. We'll have more time together."

"It's the first week of school," I say. "I get it." And really, looking back, I do get it. I don't want him to know I was worried! I feel like an idiot for thinking Rory could like someone like Gina.

"Everyone's been swamped," I say.

"More like drowning," Rory says, laughing. "Between horses, football, and school I hardly get any sleep."

"Congratulations, by the way," I say. "I heard you're starting on varsity. I'm so excited."

"Thanks. The first game is next Friday," Rory says. He scoots a little closer. "Are you going to be there?"

"I wouldn't miss it," I say.

Then he leans over and kisses me.

THE END

What's next?

CLAUDIA & *Monica*:
FRESHMAN GIRLS

Homecoming

by DIANA GALLAGHER

TURN THE PAGE FOR A SNEAK PEEK!

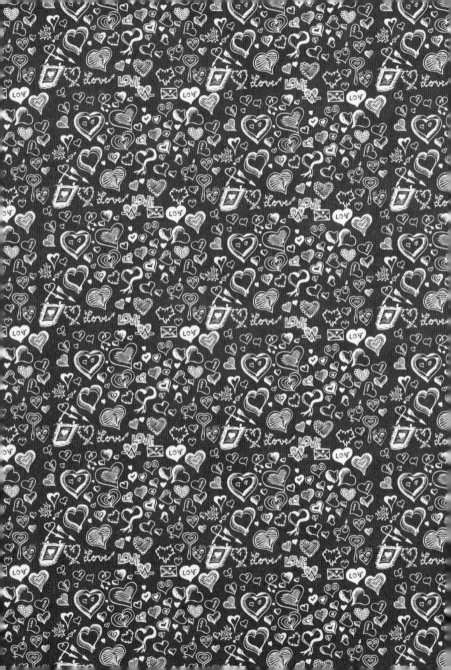

CHAPTER 1

Monica

Until I looked in my closet, I was pretty excited about Spirit Week and Homecoming. Spirit Week especially seemed fun—a whole week of hilarious and/or adorable dress-up opportunities? Yes, please!

But then I realized I have nothing to wear.

Nothing. Nada. Not a stitch.

And tomorrow is Celebrity Day.

I think of myself as a good dresser, but I'm not into fashion like some people are. As long as I look okay, and no one laughs at me, I'm happy. But Spirit Week is the perfect opportunity to burst out of ordinary into fabulous.

Too bad I don't have anything fabulous to wear, and I don't have any time to buy something fabulous to wear.

I texted Claudia fifteen minutes ago for help, and she said she'd come over.

Then I texted my best guy friend (and, okay, possibly the love of my life), Rory, to try to take my mind off clothes, but he hasn't written back.

All I can do is stare into my closet.

And worry. About what I'm going to wear, and about why Rory hasn't texted back. Usually he texts me back right away, so it's kind of weird that I haven't heard from him yet.

I send another text. Then I feel stupid. He's probably just really busy. Between football, his job, and school, Rory has a killer schedule. He hardly even has time to rehearse with his band.

Before I can waste any more time thinking about it, I hear the doorbell.

"Claudia's here!" Angela calls out.

"I'm so glad to see you!" I exclaim when Claudia walks into my room.

"What's going on?" Claudia asks. She sits on the edge of my bed.

"Nothing!" I throw up my hands. "That's the problem. I don't have a spectacular outfit for Celebrity Day, and I haven't heard from Rory."

"Maybe he's mad at you," Angela says, walking into the room. She flops on the bed next to Claudia.

"He's not mad," I say. "And I don't remember telling you to come in."

"He might be," Angela says. "And I don't remember asking."

I roll my eyes. "He's not," I say sharply. Rory and I are friends. We never fight, and everything was fine when we talked last night.

"How do you know, if you haven't heard from him?" Angela asks. That's my stepsister. She makes me crazy a lot of the time, even if we get along better now than we used to. I'm not going to bother asking her to leave. She'll just find a reason to come back or do something to make me even more annoyed. Putting up with her is easier.

"I haven't heard from Brad today either," Claudia says. That's her boyfriend, Brad Turino. They mutually crushed for a couple of years but now they're for real.

I think Rory and I might be for real, too, but I don't know. We kissed once, a few weeks ago, but since then, I've been afraid to bring it up, and we haven't had any private time together. So maybe it was a one-time thing, or maybe it was something he really regrets. I don't know.

"Is Brad mad at you?" Angela asks Claudia, shaking me out of my thoughts.

"I hope not." Claudia sighs.

"He probably has a good reason for being incommunicado," I say. "Rory is working extra hours at his job."

"Why?" Claudia asks.

I shrug. "I don't know."

"I bet he wants to get a car," Angela says, shifting her shoulders with this new know-it-all attitude she's developed since she turned ten.

"He has a car," I say. Rory calls his old Mustang a clunker, but it gets him around.

"Brad doesn't have a job," Claudia says. "So why hasn't he called or texted me?"

I start to shrug. Then my eyes fall on a framed photo on my desk. It's me, Claudia, Rory, and Brad. The guys are wearing their football uniforms, and we're all laughing. Chloe took the picture after the Pine Creek Panthers' first home game this fall.

I can't help remembering that the game was exactly a week after Rory kissed me for the first time. And only time.

"I bet they're at football practice," I say. "Since Homecoming is Friday."

"Of course!" Claudia slaps her forehead. "Coach Reynolds is making the team practice longer this week. They don't want to lose three games in a row."

"And they especially don't want to lose Pine Creek's first Homecoming game," I say.

When Pine Tree and Rock Creek were separate high schools, we always played the Homecoming game against each other. This year, the new Pine Creek team is playing Forest Lake High.

"It feels weird to be cheering with kids from Rock Creek instead of against them," Claudia says, studying the picture on my desk. "It must be really weird for the players."

"The Rock Creek kids think so too," I say. "Everyone's been on edge, according to Rory."

"Maybe the spirit points will work," Claudia says.

"What's that?" Angela asks.

"It's a contest," Claudia says. She rolls her eyes and adds, "Hence the weird outfits this week."

"We earn points for school spirit and enthusiasm," I explain. "If we make a thousand points by game time Friday, we'll get a whole day off on Monday."

"Why are they making you do it?" Angela asks.

"It's supposed to make us forget we were rivals," Claudia says.

That's not a problem for me. Rory and Chloe went to Rock Creek, and they're two of my best friends. We never let sports get in the way.

"Most of the people I talk to are okay with the new team," I say.

"The players aren't," Claudia says. "Two guys almost got benched for fighting after the last game."

"I know!" I exclaim. "Rory said they put dents in their lockers."

"Will my school get a day off too?" Angela asks.

"No, just the high school," I say.

"No fair!" Angela whines.

Claudia raises her eyebrows. "That's life," she says.

Talk about new attitudes. Ever since we started high school, Claudia acts like she thinks she's twenty-five, not fifteen.

"I bet you won't make enough points to get a

day off," Angela says. "Everybody at your school hates each other too much."

"I bet we will," I say.

"As long as nobody gets into a fistfight or anything," Claudia adds.

"We get extra points for dressing up every day," I say. "Tomorrow is Celebrity Day."

"Cool!" Angela says.

"We can dress like anyone who's famous," I explain.

"I'm wearing a sundress and a denim jacket like Sky Taylor," Claudia says.

"Sky has blond hair," Angela says. "Yours is black."

"But it's long and curly like Sky's hair," Claudia says. She looks at me. "Hey, Mon, that reminds me. Can I borrow your cowgirl boots for my outfit tomorrow?"

"Absolutely," I say. "You can't be Sky without boots."

"What's Chloe wearing?" Claudia asks.

"Her horse show riding clothes," I say.

Claudia looks puzzled. "What celebrity is that?"

"Mia Slade," I say.

Claudia frowns. "Mia Slade? From *City Girls*?"

I nod. "Mia's first movie was *Horses and Hearts*, like ten years ago," I explain.

"Never heard of it," Claudia says.

"Nobody has except Chloe," I say, smiling. Chloe can be kind of . . . out of it sometimes. But I like that about her. She's not like everyone else.

"Who are you going to be?" Angela asks me.

"I don't know," I say.

"Go as Princess Patsy!" Angela exclaims. I guess she's not too old for some of her kiddy stuff. She's been obsessed with Princess Patsy basically as long as I've known her. "She's a celebrity."

A celebrity is a famous person that everybody knows, so that was true. But I'd wear my grandpa's old paint-splattered coveralls before I'd show up at school in ribbons and layers of pink gauze like a Princess Patsy doll!

Claudia saves me with a better suggestion. "Go as Haley Hover. She's your favorite."

Haley Hover is a singing sensation with a flair for off-beat fashion. Everything about her screams, "I'm gorgeous, amazing, and famous!" But my wardrobe mutters, "Ninth grade, off the rack, won't get grounded for wearing it."

"Nothing in my closet is as glamorous as the things Haley Hover wears," I say. "I can't afford that kind of clothes."

"She's not always that glamorous," Claudia reminds me. She points to the poster on my wall. "Look."

It's my favorite photo of Haley. She's wearing jeans and a T-shirt with a cool design on it and sparkly flats. It's such a cute outfit. And when I look down, I realize I'm wearing almost exactly the same thing. I just need some sparkles on my shoes.

"I can do that," I say, smiling. "Thanks!"

Suddenly my phone plays my all-time favorite Haley Hover song. "Lost in your love, there's no way out . . ." That means I have a text message from Rory.

I'll call u later!

About the Author

Diana G. Gallagher lives in Florida with five dogs, four cats, and a cranky parrot. Her hobbies are gardening, garage sales, and grandchildren. She has been an English equitation instructor, a professional folk musician, and an artist. However, she had aspirations to be a professional writer at the age of twelve. She has written dozens of books for kids and young adults. Her bestselling Claudia Cristina Cortez and Monica books are available from Stone Arch Books.